# Reading Together

# Give Me My Yam!

# Read it together

*Give Me My Yam!* is a story set in the Caribbean and told in the gentle, rhythmical style of a traditional folktale.

The patterns and tuneful quality of this story make it ideal for reading aloud.

"Mmmm," thought Jordan. "This will tas delicious with a nice piece of brown stewed chicken."

Look at the fish leap out of the river!

Did Jordan catch it?

Talking about the book with children is a good way to get them involved in the story and helps to make them into thoughtful readers.

The story might remind you of *This Is the House That Jack Built* because of the way the events build on each other. This strong pattern really helps children to join in and take on the reading for themselves.

As well as being a story, *Give Me My Yam!* is a kind of memory game. Children can learn to retell the story really well, and begin to take on the different voices of each character.

Your child will enjoy talking about the story, both during the reading and afterwards. They might want to tell it in their own words.

We hope you enjoy reading this book together.

To Little Buffalo,
from Mama Buffalo
J.B.

To my niece, Robyn
P.M.

First published 1998 by Walker Books Ltd
87 Vauxhall Walk, London SE11 5HJ

2 4 6 8 10 9 7 5 3 1

Text © 1998 Jan Blake
Illustrations © 1998 Peter Melnyczuk
Introductory and concluding notes © 1998 CLPE

Printed in Great Britain

ISBN 0-7445-4885-3

# Give Me My Yam!

## Retold by
## Jan Blake

## Illustrated by
## Peter Melnyczuk

WALKER BOOKS
AND SUBSIDIARIES
LONDON · BOSTON · SYDNEY

Jordan loved to eat yams.
One day he took his
spade and dug and dug.
He found a nice fat yam.
He took his fat yam
down to the river Denzo to
wash it clean, clean, clean.

"Mmmm," thought Jordan. "This will taste delicious with a nice piece of brown stewed chicken."

The river Denzo snatched his
fat yam out of his hand
and carried it away.

Jordan put his hands on his hips
and cried,
*"Denzo, Denzo, give me my yam,
the yam that I found
on my mother's farm."*

The river Denzo gave Jordan
a big fat fish.

Jordan walked home with his big fat fish.
"Mmm," thought Jordan. "This will taste
nice with some boiled green bananas."

A great hawk swooped down and
snatched his big fat fish out of his hand
and carried it away.

Jordan put his hands on his hips
and cried,

*"Hawk, Hawk, give me my fish,*
*the fish that Denzo gave me,*
*Denzo who took my yam,*
*the yam that I found on my*
*mother's farm."*

The hawk gave Jordan
a beautiful tail feather.

Jordan walked home with his feather.
"Hmmm," thought Jordan. "I don't
imagine this will taste very nice,
but it looks nice and it feels soft.
I'll give this to my mum."

The wind blew harder and harder and snatched his feather out of his hand.

Jordan put his hands on his hips and cried,
*"Wind, Wind, give me my feather,
the feather that the hawk gave me,
the hawk that took my fish,
the fish that Denzo gave me,
Denzo who took my yam,
the yam that I found on my
mother's farm."*

The wind gave Jordan
a multi-coloured leaf.

"Hmm," thought Jordan. "I can't eat a leaf. I know, I'll press it in a book."

A goat snatched the leaf out of
his hand and gobbled it up.

Jordan put his hands on his hips
and cried,
*"Goat, Goat, give me my leaf,*
*the leaf that the wind gave me,*
*the wind that took my feather,*
*the feather that the hawk gave me,*
*the hawk that took my fish,*
*the fish that Denzo gave me,*
*Denzo who took my yam,*
*the yam that I found on my*
*mother's farm."*

The goat let Jordan milk her.
He had a calabash full of
fresh creamy goat's milk.

Jordan walked home with the milk.
"Mmmmmm," he thought.
"I love goat's milk. I'll share this
with my mum and dad."

But he didn't see the tree root
growing out of the ground, and before
he could stop himself he was tumbling
and falling and the calabash was
sailing through the air.
They both landed – CRASH!

Jordan put his hands on his hips
and cried,
*"Tree, Tree, give me my milk,*
*the milk that the goat gave me,*
*the goat that ate my leaf,*
*the leaf that the wind gave me,*
*the wind that took my feather,*
*the feather that the hawk gave me,*
*the hawk that took my fish,*
*the fish that Denzo gave me,*
*Denzo who took my yam,*
*the yam that I found on my*
*mother's farm."*

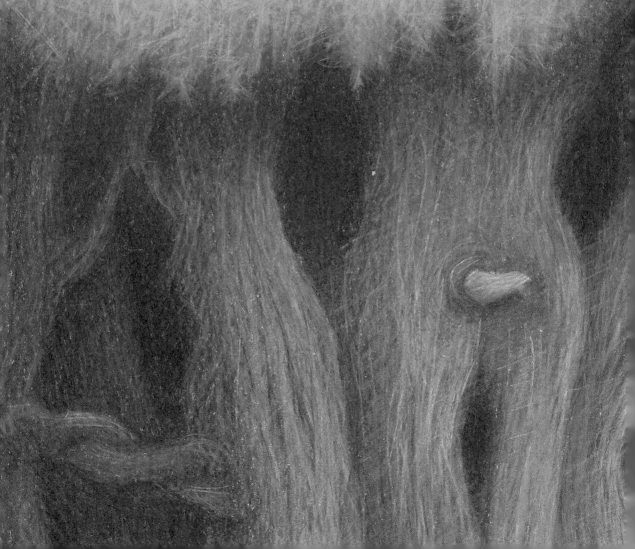

The tree looked hard at Jordan
and said, "Look behind me."
Jordan looked behind the tree
and found a spade.

"Dig there," said the tree.
So Jordan dug and dug
and what do you think
he found?

A yam, a nice fat yam,
which he took to the river Denzo
and washed clean, clean, clean.
He ran all the way home and handed
it to his mother who peeled it and
cooked it and gave it to him with
some brown stewed chicken.

# Delicious!

# Read it again

### Lost and found
Children could tell their own stories of finding treasure or losing something precious, which might be based on a real life event or completely imaginary.

### Market stall
You could help your child to create their own market stall with a variety of fruit and vegetables borrowed from the kitchen. Labels with names and prices could be added to make the shopping games more fun.

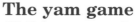

He dug and dug and found a box, and in the box...

### The yam game
Children can play the yam game (*opposite*) to get to know the story and enjoy it even more.
You just need a dice and a counter for each player.

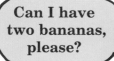

Can I have two bananas, please?

Yes. And anything else?

1. Throw an even number to find a nice fat yam and start.

2.

3. The river Denzo snatches the yam. Follow it to 6.

4.

8. A great hawk swoops down and snatches the fish. Stay until you throw 4, 5 or 6.

7.

6.

5. The river Denzo gives you a big fat fish. Miss a turn while you think how to eat it.

9.

10. Run back a space to catch the hawk's beautiful tail feather.

11. The wind snatches the feather. You are blown to 15. The other players go back 3 spaces.

12.

16. The goat eats your leaf, but lets you milk her. Stay a turn.

15.

14. The wind gives you a multi-coloured leaf. Go to 15.

13.

17. The fresh creamy goat's milk is spilled! Go back to 13.

18.

19. You dig under the tree. Go forward one space.

20. You find a yam, a nice fat yam. HURRAY! YOU'VE WON!

# Reading Together

The *Reading Together* series is divided into four levels – starting with red, then on to yellow, blue and finally green. The six books in each level offer children varied experiences of reading. There are stories, poems, rhymes and songs, traditional tales and information books to choose from.

Accompanying the series is a Parents' Handbook, which looks at all the different ways children learn to read and explains how *your* help can really make a difference!

     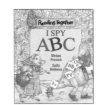